HOT DOG and BOB

and the Exceptionally Eggy Attack of the ███████ ██ters

BY **L. Bob Rovetch**   ILLUSTRATED BY **Dave Whamond**

chronicle books · san francisco

For the *other* Mr. G.—Guthrie Savage Friedman the Great —L. R.

Book design by Mary Beth Fiorentino.
Typeset in Clarendon and Agenda.
The illustrations in this book were rendered in ink,
watercolor washes and Prismacolor.
Manufactured in China.

Library of Congress Cataloging-in-Publication Data
Rovetch, Lissa.
Hot Dog and Bob and the exceptionally eggy attack of the Game
Gators : adventure #4 / by L. Bob Rovetch ; illustrated by Dave Whamond.
p. cm.
Summary: When all of the fifth-graders from Lugenheimer Elementary
School are transported to the domain of the rapping Game Gator to
compete in life-or-death games, it is up to Bob,
his best friend Clementine, and superhero Hot Dog from the
planet Dogzalot to rescue them.
ISBN-13: 978-0-8118-5603-4 (library edition)
ISBN-10: 0-8118-5603-8 (library edition)
ISBN-13: 978-0-8118-5604-1 (pbk.)
ISBN-10: 0-8118-5604-6 (pbk)
[1. Alligators—Fiction. 2. Games—Fiction. 3. Frankfurters—Fiction.
4. Extraterrestrial beings—Fiction. 5. Schools—Fiction.
6. Humorous stories.]   I. Whamond, Dave, ill. II. Title.
PZ7.R784Hos 2007
[Fic]—dc22
2006014858

Distributed in Canada by Raincoast Books
9050 Shaughnessy Street, Vancouver, British Columbia V6P 6E5

10 9 8 7 6 5 4 3 2 1

Chronicle Books LLC
680 Second Street, San Francisco, California 94107

www.chroniclekids.com

Contents

Chapter 1

Recess

The first time Hot Dog popped out of my lunch
box, I was surprised. When he said I'd been
picked to be his Earth partner, I was even more
surprised. When he said we were going to be
saving the world from scary space aliens,
I switched from surprised to terrified!

My name's Bob. I'm in the fifth grade at
Lugenheimer Elementary, and I have the
weirdest life! In just the last couple of months
I've battled psycho hypno hamsters, pointy
pencil people, and an extremely unfriendly
pizza person.

It wasn't my choice. The job totally got chosen for me by the Big Bun. She's the leader of Dogzalot, a peace-loving planet full of superhero hot dogs who get beamed across the solar system to stop evil aliens and make the universe a safer place.

"Hey, Marco," I said to my friend at recess. "You haven't seen Clementine anywhere, have you?"

"Dude! I think I lost her!" said Marco.

"Yeah, right!" I laughed.

"No, I'm not kidding!" said Marco. "We were shootin' hoops on the blacktop, and I turned my back for a millisecond, and she completely disappeared!"

"Okay," I said calmly, "exactly what do you mean by *disappeared?*"

"I mean *dis-ap-peared!*" said Marco, "as in abracadabra, now you see her, now you don't!"

"Oh, she probably just went to get a drink of water," I told Marco.

But I knew Clementine would never just walk out in the middle of a basketball game. Clementine's not the type to walk out on anything. I mean, other than her bad habit of eating unbelievably disgusting sandwiches at lunch, she's basically the coolest person I know.

She's helped Hot Dog and me deal with every alien attack so far. Plus, since Hot Dog sprays forgetting mist at the end of every mission, Clementine's the only one besides me who has any memory at all of the bizarre alien invasions that keep happening at our school.

Have you ever had a bad feeling? You know, the kind that ties your stomach up in knots? You know, the kind that almost instantly changes from a little bad feeling into a big bad actual thing?

If you answered no, then I'm happy for you— really I am! It's so nice that you've lived such a wonderfully easy life. You're probably the best-looking, most talented, most popular person in your entire school, and you'll probably grow up to be a famous actor or the president of the United States—or both.

But if you answered yes, if you know what it feels like to have a few little nervous butterflies in your belly turn into an army of killer bees, then you can relate to how I felt when Marco vanished right in the middle of our conversation!

"Marco?" I called out all over the place. "Come on, quit messing around!"

But there was no Marco!

"Hey, Bob!" said Ricardo. "Have you seen Danny? He was goalie on our soccer team, and he just totally split!"

Before long every kid in my class was either missing or looking for someone. Was this some twisted game of hide-and-seek or—? I didn't want to think about it. One minute we were all running around, calling out for our missing friends. And the next minute I was totally and completely by myself!

"Hello?" I said. "Anybody out there? Come out, come out, wherever you are! Okay, guys, that was a good one! Joke's on me! I lose! Game's over!"

"Oh, on the contrary," said a loud, creepy voice. "This game has just begun!"

The Game

Something reached up from the blacktop,
grabbed my shoes and yanked me underground.
I was falling through a big dark tube. I was
crashing down a never-ending pretzel-shaped
slide! If I hadn't been so sure I was gonna die,
it would have been an awesome ride. But since
I was pretty positive I *was* gonna die . . .

I shot out of the tube, crashed into a wall and
landed spread-eagle on the ground. When my
head finally stopped spinning, I got my next
big shock. The wall I'd crashed into wasn't really
a wall at all. It was an egg. A *really big* egg!

"Greetings, Player Two," said a voice. "And welcome to the Gator Game!"

"The what?" I asked, looking around to see who was talking.

"The Gator Game," the voice repeated. "If you beat Player One, you will go on to compete in my Intergalactic Gator Game Championships! But if you lose—*bwa-ha-ha!*"

"*Bwa-ha-ha?*" I asked nervously.

"*Bwa-ha-ha,*" said the voice, "is Gator talk for 'this game has only one winner, so if you value your life, you might not want to lose.'"

I had a bunch of questions: Where am I? Who are you? What have you done with my friends? and If I'm Player Two, then who's Player One?

But before I could ask any of them, the underground room went crazy. Buzzers buzzed, bells rang, whistles whistled, lights flashed and earsplitting music blasted all around. If I wasn't freaked out, it would have been cool.

"The object of the game," said the voice, "is to make it to the finish line before Player One—"

"That's it?" I thought to myself. "That doesn't sound so hard."

"Without getting caught by my little Game Gator here," the voice continued, "who should be hatching . . . right about . . . NOW!"

The huge egg started to rumble and crack. BLAMMO! It exploded into a billion pieces, and a big reptilian creature busted out. I saw two exit signs flashing over two doorways. I picked one and ran for it.

Meet Player One

I was running for my life down a soggy dark tunnel, but I wasn't running fast enough. *Squishy-squooshy, squishy-squooshy*—the Game Gator was getting closer and closer, and there was still no sign of Hot Dog anywhere! My mind was racing. Why wasn't he showing up? Where in the world could he be? What if he decided to give up being a superhero? If I had to play this so-called game on my own, I was such dead meat!

"HOT DOGGGG!" I yelled as I ran. "HELLLLLP MEEEEEE!"

But Hot Dog didn't show. For all I knew, I was never going to see him, or anyone else, ever again!

"Oh, forget it!" I panted. "What good is a stinkin' superhero partner if he's not there when you need him, anyway?"

Right then I saw a ray of light shining down from a hole up above. *Squishy-squooshy*—the slimy sounds were getting closer.

I jumped toward the light, grabbed on to the opening at the top of the tunnel and pulled myself up. I held my breath and waited for the *squishy-squooshy* sounds to get quieter. When I was sure the Game Gator had lost my scent, I breathed a gigantic sigh of relief.

Other than a messy pile of junk in the corner, the room I'd ended up in was straight out of a king's palace. There was fancy velvet and gold stuff all over the place, and right in the middle of the room was another egg. It was just like the last one, only bigger!

"Fancy meeting you here!" said Clementine.

"Clementine?" I said. "How did you—? I mean, when did you—? I mean, this egg! We have to get away from this egg!"

"No joke, Einstein!" said Clementine. "You should have seen the critter that hatched out of one of those things and chased me. It was fast *and ugly!*"

"That's exactly what happened to me!" I said. "Wait! Don't tell me . . . *you're* Player One!"

"And *you're* Player Two?" She gasped. "Bob! This is a disaster! Whichever one of us makes it to the finish line first gets out of here alive. But the other one, the loser—"

I didn't wait for the end of her sentence.

"I'm too young to die!" I panicked.

"What about me?" said Clementine. "I'm three whole months younger than you are!"

"You are not!" I argued. "I'm three months younger than you are! Look, we don't have time

to fight about this stupid stuff. We have to do
something—*now!*"

"Wait! I think I've got it!" said Clementine.
"What if we make up our own rules? If we play
as a team, we can both reach the finish line at
the very same time!"

"Perfect!" I agreed. "That way there won't be any losers!"

"Exactly," said Clementine. "Only winners!"

But before we could make a move, the buzzers, bells, whistles and music went off all over again. The gigantic egg was glowing. The gigantic egg was rumbling. . . .

Chapter 4

Mr. G.

KABLAM! The gigantic egg blew wide open like a red-hot volcano! And out of the fiery flames stepped the freakiest alien we'd met so far! We were amazed to see the biggest alligator in the universe breaking out of that egg, but when he opened his mouth to talk, we were speechless!

> *"I'm Mister G., and I'm here to say*
> *The Gator Game is fun to play.*
> *But tell me, what is wrong with you fools?*
> *Who gave you permission to break my rules?"*

Mr. G. rapped like a rap star and might have even kind of been cool. That is, if he hadn't been—well—an extraterrestrial alligator!

"Uh-oh," Clementine whispered. "He's onto our plan!"

Mr. G. must have overheard Clementine because the next thing he rapped was

>*"There's no teamin' up in the Gator Game!*
>*You cheatin' fools are the ones to blame!*
>*If being friends is what you choose,*
>*Then you're both just gonna have to lose!"*

"Wait! You have it all wrong!" Clementine said, thinking fast. "We're not friends! As a matter of fact, Player Two and I hate each other's guts!"

"*And* muscles and bones and nerves and arteries!" I added helpfully.

"Why—I wouldn't be friends with Player Two if he were the last person on Earth!" Clementine went on. "Just look at this skinny little weasel! His knees are bony, his ears are funny, not to mention the fact that he's a terrible dresser!"

"And you can't believe how much I hate Player One's guts!" I chimed in. "Oh, sure, she might look kind of cute on the outside, but underneath she's mean as all get-out! Plus she eats *really* gross sandwiches! If I *were* looking to team up with somebody, Player One would be my way, way, *way* last choice!"

Clementine and I winked at each other and crossed our fingers. If we were lucky, Mr. G. would never guess that we were just trying to fake him out. Unfortunately, it wasn't our lucky day.

He said,

"Nobody messes with Mr. G!

Did you think that you could outsmart me?

Without a loser this game's no fun.

So you can say good-bye. Your days are done!"

Chapter 5

Swamped

A trapdoor opened right under our feet and sucked us down another crazy slide.

"Would you please get your shoe out of my ear?" shouted Clementine. "And where the heck is that flying weenie when we need him?"

"Why don't you get your ear out of my shoe?" I yelled back as we fell. "And I hate to say this, but I'm starting to think that Hot Dog might not be coming this time."

"Bummer!" Clementine shouted. "By the way, I really didn't appreciate those snotty remarks you made about me back there!"

"*My* snotty remarks?" I yelled. "What do you call 'skinny little weasel' with 'bony' knees and 'funny' ears—a compliment?"

But before Clementine could argue back, we shot out the bottom of the slide into a *freezing cold swamp!*

"AAAHHH!!!" We screamed, sputtered and splashed toward the shore (which was at least five or six zillion miles away).

CHATTER

CHATTER

"Look, a log!" I yelled out.

We grabbed on to the slimy, floating log and gasped for air. Then, all of a sudden, the log splashed out of the water, opened its mouth and started chasing us around the swamp!

"AAAHHH!!!" We screamed again.

"That's not a log!" hollered Clementine.

"No kidding!" I said, swallowing a mouthful of gross green pond water.

Then, just as the slimy jaws of death were closing in on us . . .

"Never fear! Hot Dog is here!" Hot Dog shouted, zooming up in a speedboat. "Unless you two guppies wanna be gator grub, you'd better get your booties in this boaty!"

Clementine and I climbed aboard as fast as we could. The Game Gator tried to catch us, but Hot Dog put the pedal to the metal and outran the slimy sucker!

"Thanks!" I panted when we got to shore. "I was afraid you'd forgotten about us!"

"Me? Forget about you?" said Hot Dog. "No way, partner! The Big Bun and the Dogzalot scientists were having technical difficulties beaming me down here. Turns out Mr. G. put a beam-proof barrier around this whole underground area."

"Well, you finally made it, and that's what matters," said Clementine. "Now if you wouldn't mind getting us out of this slime pit . . ."

"I would if I could," said Hot Dog, "but I'm afraid we're in a bit of a pickle."

"Why am I not surprised?" groaned Clementine.

"The Dogzalot scientists figured out how to break through the barrier coming down here," said Hot Dog, "but not vice versa."

"Vice versa?" I asked.

"As long as Mr. G's around," Hot Dog sighed, "nobody's gettin' outta this place!"

"In other words," said Clementine, "this game isn't over at all!"

And boy was she ever right! Just then another trapdoor opened under us and sucked us down another insane slide!

Chapter 6

Eggs

"Whoa, baby!" Hot Dog hollered. "I'm too old for carnival rides!"

"How old are you, anyway?" Clementine said as we fell.

"Oh, we don't give much thought to age on Dogzalot," he said as we spiraled down, bumping pinball style. "Two, maybe three? You guys know what a lousy memory I have. I guess I mighta, sorta, kinda lost track."

"No offense," I yelled, "but if you can't even remember whether you're two or three years old, your memory must be *really* bad!"

"Not two or three *years!*" laughed Hot Dog. "Two or three *hundred* years!"

"No way!" I said. "How is that even possible?"

I had so many questions to ask Hot Dog: Is everyone on Dogzalot born with superhero powers? Do hot dogs go to school? And what does the Big Bun look like? I mean, does everyone just call her that? Or is she really— you know—a great big bun?

But before I could ask, we plopped off the slide and landed right in front of Mr. G., who said,

"Well, isn't this a nice surprise!

I can hardly believe my eyes!

You made it out of my swamp I see.

And brought a juicy little snack for me!"

Hot Dog stood up superhero style and said, "I'm no snack, Mack! Now remove that beam barrier on the double, and let us out, or you're in trouble!"

"Maybe you should leave the rhyming to the experts," I whispered to Hot Dog.

If Mr. G. was scared of Hot Dog, he sure
didn't show it. He walked over to a big red
curtain and pulled it open. Every kid from
my class was there, and they were all trapped
in see-through egg jails!

The whole horrible scene (with our friends in eggs and the red curtain and everything) seemed so much more like some kind of freaky play than real life that Clementine and I just stood there and stared.

After way too long I finally yelled, "Don't worry, Marco! We'll get you out of that thing!"

Every now and then, Clementine says stuff without thinking it all the way through. "That's it! You rotten rhyming slimy head!" she yelled at Mr. G. "You let our friends go, or else!" But Mr. G. didn't seem too scared. He just snapped his fingers, and all of a sudden Clementine was stuck in an egg jail too. Things were going from terribly bad to horribly worse fast!

The ceiling slid open, and Mr. G. *and* all of
my egg-trapped classmates started floating up.
Mr. G. waved down to Hot Dog and me and said,

> **"This planet is as boring as it can be,**
> **So I'm takin' these eggs back home with me.**
> **On Gator-Ville, folks have more fun.**
> **So ciao for now, 'cause I gotta run!"**

"Quick!" I said to Hot Dog. "Fly up and do
your stuff!"

"Hang on, kiddos!" Hot Dog called. "Help is
on the way!"

Hot Dog put his arms up, Superman style.
Only he wasn't going anywhere. Neither of us
was! Our feet were permanently stuck to the
ground!

"Well, whaddya know about that?!" said
Hot Dog. "I sure as onions didn't see that one
comin'! By golly! That Mr. G. sure is one sneaky
old gator!"

"We have to do something!" I screamed. "We
have to stop him! We have to save Clementine!"

Chapter 7

Oops!

"They don't call me a superhero for nothin'!" Hot Dog said, pushing one of his secret bun buttons. "Say good-bye, Mr. G., " 'cause you, my friend, are goin' down!"

The good thing was that Hot Dog's bun button worked, and gallons of yellow mustard squirted out. The bad thing was that he totally missed his target! The mustard flew right by Mr. G. and smothered one of his floating eggs instead. The egg (and the person inside it) came crashing down to the ground.

"Oops!" said Hot Dog.

"Oops is right!" I said. "Hot Dog, you have to unstick our feet so we can help whoever's in that smashed-up egg!"

"This should do the trick!" said Hot Dog.

He pushed another bun button, and sauerkraut shot out all over our feet!

"Yuck! That stuff stinks!" I said. "Couldn't you have picked some less disgusting topping?"

"Nope," Hot Dog said, lifting up a foot. "Sauerkraut's the ticket, partner. You see, on Dogzalot we make this stuff with special vinegar that's so strong the acid in it will dissolve darn near anything ya got!"

The chemistry lesson was interesting, but I had other things on my mind. I pulled my feet out of the goo and ran over to the broken egg.

"Hey, loser!" said the person in the egg. "Hurry up and get me outta here!"

"Oh, no!" I whined to Hot Dog. "Of all the kids in my whole class, you had to pick this one to shoot down?"

I know it sounds like a jerky thing to say, but the guy on the ground, the guy who called me a loser—that guy was Barfalot, the dirty, rotten bully who totally has it out for me!

"Bob, I can't move!" Barfalot moaned. "Please, I beg of you! Help me out here! Give me a hand!"

But when I reached out to help him, he just splashed mustard in my face and laughed like a maniac.

"Ha, ha! What a sucker!" he snorted. "That was great! Man, you're such an idiot!"

"You wanna know what I think, pal?" said Hot Dog. "I think somebody oughta teach you some manners! That's what I think!"

"Oh, yeah?" said Barfalot. "I'd like to see ya try!"

"Oh, yeah?" said Hot Dog.

"Yeah!" said Barfalot.

With all of the action down on the ground, we'd forgotten all about the action up in the air.

"Um, I could be wrong," I said, "but I'm pretty sure manners are the last thing we need to worry about right now."

Mr. G. and his floating eggs had almost reached the giant hole in the ceiling. If they made it through the opening and out into space, we'd never see them again!

Chapter 8

Best Friends

"I'll deal with you later," Hot Dog told Barfalot. "Right now I've got bigger fish to fry!"

Barfalot didn't say a thing. He usually had Pigburt and Slugburt (his brainless bodyguard brothers) to back him up. But seeing as they were stuck in eggs, they couldn't really help him out too much. Besides, I could tell by the look on Barfalot's face that he was pretty busy just trying to figure out what Hot Dog would want with fried fish anyway.

Hot Dog flew all over the place, and so did his hands. Watching him push all his bun

buttons was like watching a master musician

play the piano. Ketchup, onions, pickle relish

and sesame seeds squirted out as he flew.

I don't know why the goopy mixture stuck

together to form a temporary ceiling. But

I do know that the huge opening was filled

just in time!

Mr. G. and his egg prisoners floated up to Hot Dog's homemade ceiling and stuck there just like flies on flypaper.

Hot Dog dusted off his tiny hands, smoothed out his cape and said, "Well, Mr. G., I guess playtime's over!"

I've had a lot of surprises lately but nothing like the one that came next.

Barfalot grabbed a rope from a pile of junk in the corner and shouted, "Hey, Mr. G., catch this, and I'll yank ya down!"

All those times we thought Barfalot was ditching class he must have been training for the rodeo, 'cause he threw that rope exactly like a champion cowboy throws his lasso. Mr. G. caught it on the first try and was down in a flash.

"Hi, I'm Barfalot, and you're the coolest guy I've ever met!" Barfalot said, shaking Mr. G.'s hand. "Can I be your friend and play fun games with you forever and ever and ever?"

Mr. G. was so happy he looked like he was going to cry. He put his big, scaly arm around Barfalot and said,

"You are my main man, Mr. B.!

The new best friend of Mr. G.!

At last—someone who likes to play!

The rest of you can go away!"

He snapped his fingers, and all the other eggs came crashing down.

"Ouch! That smarts!" said Felicia.

"Whoa!" said Marco. "That was a totally radical wipeout!"

"Where am I?" asked Danny and a bunch of other kids.

Everybody was moaning and groaning from the fall, but they all seemed amazingly okay. They were sore and confused—but alive. I was glad my classmates were all right—even Pigburt and Slugburt, who just kept saying, "Cool ride! Can we do it again?"

"Hey, buddy!" Hot Dog called from across the room, "I think you'd better come over here."

He didn't have to say another word. I knew something had happened to Clementine, and I knew it wasn't good.

Chapter 9

So Long, Clementine

"NOOOO!!!" I wailed when I saw Clementine. She wasn't moving at all. She was just lying there. She wasn't even breathing.

"She can't be . . . !" I said.

Hot Dog put his hand gently on top of mine and looked right into my eyes.

"Sometimes these things happen, partner," he said, shaking his head. "Sometimes bad things happen to good people."

"Come on, Clementine. You're too young to die!" I cried. "Please, Clem! Quit kidding around and wake up! Wait, I know! I'll make you a deal.

You be okay, and I'll eat ten of those disgusting sandwiches that you're always begging me to try at lunch! Here, I'll even write it down so you know I mean it!"

I dumped out my pockets and found an old candy wrapper and a chewed-up pencil. Here's what I wrote:

I, Bob, hereby promise to eat ten entire disgusting sandwiches made by Clementine, if she promises not to die.

Looking back on it now, I'm sure I could have come up with a better deal than that. Looking back on it now, I *really* wish I had. But for some reason Clementine's creative lunchtime concoctions were the only things I could think of. I folded my promise, stuck it in her pocket and prayed.

Donkey Dandruff

"Forget it, kid," said Hot Dog. "Bargaining ain't gonna bring her back—*I am!*"

"What?" I asked, hopeful and doubtful at the same time. "Did you just say what I think you just said?"

Hot Dog pushed a tiny shiny white bun button that I'd never seen him use before.

"It's time," he announced, "for the *flakes of life!*"

It was amazing! The most magical sparkling white crystals fell from his bun like snowflakes from the sky.

"Wow!" I said. "It's so beautiful!"

"I know," Hot Dog agreed. "It's sparkly donkey dandruff."

"Wait a minute!" I said. "My best friend in the entire world is totally dead, and you're covering her with donkey dandruff?"

But that was the last complaint Hot Dog heard out of my mouth. I know it doesn't make any sense, but the flakes of life actually worked! Clementine wiggled her nose, opened her eyes, stood up and sneezed all over me!

"Clementine!" I said, throwing my arms around her, "you're alive!"

"Of course I'm alive," she said, dusting off the donkey dandruff. "What in the world is this stuff all over me?"

"No time for small talk, little lady," Hot Dog said, pointing across the room. "We got a little business to take care of first!"

Chapter 10

See Ya Later, Alligator

We knew Mr. G. was smart. We just didn't know *how* smart. In the time it took Hot Dog to bring Clementine back to life, Mr. G. had built a rocket ship. It was big, it was bad, and it was pointing right at the patched-up ceiling!

Mr. G. was sitting in the pilot's seat, and guess who was sitting in the chair next to him? Mr. G. rolled down the cockpit window and said,

"Well, when I came down here to have some fun,

I was more alone than most anyone!

Nobody liked me, but I didn't care,

'Cause when you're all alone, you don't have to share!

65

But then a miracle happened to me.

I got a best friend called Mr. B.!

Good riddance, Earthlings! You can all chill!

'Cause we're goin' back home to Gator-Ville!"

Then he revved up his engines and waved good-bye to us.

"Hmm, no more Barfalot?" said Clementine. "I don't think I have a problem with that. How about you, Bob?"

"Hmm, let's see," I said. "We get rid of the rhyming reptile *and* the bully at the same time? That works for me!"

"Not so fast!" said Hot Dog. "The Big Bun sent me on this mission to rescue and protect *all* human beings, *including* the dirty, rotten meanies! I'm sorry to say this, Mr. G., but your new best friend's stayin' here with me!"

"Yeah! That's right!" Pigburt chimed in. "Nobody steals Barfalot!"

"Yeah! That's right!" Slugburt repeated. "Nobody steals Barfalot!"

I have to admit I was impressed. Barfalot's
brainless brothers scrambled up the side of the
rocket ship, squeezed through the open window
and—well, to be honest, that was pretty much
the end of the impressive part. Once they made
it into the cockpit, Mr. G. just rolled up his
window, and instead of one new friend, now
he had three.

Chapter 11

Singin' in the Rain

Hot Dog put his hands up to his mouth, megaphone style, and yelled, "Release the humans! I repeat, release the humans!"

"Oh, come on, Hot Dog," Clementine begged. "Can't we please just let him keep them? I mean, just think how much better off this world would be without those terrible troublemaking triplets!"

"Now I know you don't really mean that, Miss Clementine," said Hot Dog. "I know that *you* know that there's a little bit o' good in each and every one of us!"

"I do?" Clementine asked.

"Sure you do!" said Hot Dog. "Why else do you think the Big Bun chose you to be my Earth partner's partner?"

"She *chose* me?" asked Clementine. "You mean it's not just some terrible coincidence that I keep getting mixed up in all of this freaky alien stuff?"

"Trust me, darlin'!" said Hot Dog. "When it comes to the Big Bun, there *are* no coincidences! Now come on, you two! Let's make this wrong a *right!*"

Clementine and I still weren't a hundred percent convinced. But we couldn't let Hot Dog down.

"Okay, I guess I'm in," sighed Clementine.

"Me, too," I said. "But you'd better hurry up and tell us the plan before they get away!"

"Tell you the *plant?*" Hot Dog asked. "Well, I never had much of a green thumb myself, but I like lookin' at a nice plant as much as the next

guy—leafy plants, flowery plants, poky plants.
And, hey—speakin' of plants, you
think you got some good-lookin'
plants here on *this* planet? You
should *see* some of the plants we
got growin' up there on Dogzalot!"

"What in the world is he talking about?" asked
Clementine. "Am I missing something here?"

"Not *plant!*" I yelled at Hot Dog. "*Plan!*
They're getting away! We need to stop them!
You have to tell us the *plan!*"

"Oh! The plan!" Hot Dog exclaimed. "Well, why didn't you say so in the first place?"

"Oh, thank goodness!" sighed Clementine. "You had me pretty worried for a minute there, Hot Dog!"

"Yes siree, Bobby Boy," Hot Dog rambled on. "We need a plan! That's for sure! Be prepared, I always say! Why do you think I always carry my umbrella around? Because I'm prepared—that's why!"

Then he pulled an umbrella out of his bun and started singing and dancing like he was the star of his very own Broadway musical:

"Oh, I'm singin' in the rain, just singin' in the rain.

What a glorious feeling, I'm happy again!"

Up until then Hot Dog had been acting fairly normal (for a hot dog, that is). And with everything else that was going on, I'd forgotten all about his memory problem. The first time

I met Hot Dog, he told me how it happened.
He'd bumped his head on Rocky Rock Monster's
fists of granite. That was *supposedly* why the
Big Bun beamed Hot Dog into my lunch box
in the first place. Since I had a pretty good
memory and all, I was chosen to be Hot Dog's
partner here on Earth—just until his memory
got better. Which, judging from the umbrella
act, was not happening anytime soon.

So there we were, trapped underground with our dancing hot dog, our dazed and confused classmates and a rocket ship that had to be stopped.

"Well," I said to Clementine, "I guess it's up to you and me."

"Are you out of your mind?" Clementine yelled at me.

"Probably," I answered. "Come on, let's go!"

Chapter 12

Crazy Brave Bob

If I'd stopped to think about it, I never would have done it. It was like regular boring Bob went on a vacation and crazy brave Bob just kind of took over!

I grabbed an old bike frame and an inner tube from the big junk pile in the corner and made a heavy-duty slingshot.

"It's a long shot," I said, "but maybe if we jam up the jet-propulsion unit, they won't be able to take off!"

"It's worth a try," said Clementine. "And we can use these things for ammunition!"

The *things* she was talking about were the heavy broken pieces of thick shell from Mr. G.'s shattered egg prisons. They were perfect for the job. We shot them one after the other right into the rocket ship's jet-propulsion unit. And believe it or not, the engines shut down!

SPROING OING OING!

"We did it!" I cheered.

"Sorry, Mr. G.!" Clementine shouted. "You are officially grounded!"

But Mr. G. didn't look too upset. He just revved up his engines all over again. And this time he was really taking off!

Chapter 12½

Singin' in More Rain

The rockets blasted flames right at us. The heat from their fire was unbearable. And here's the weird thing. With everything that was going on, Hot Dog didn't seem worried at all! He just went on with his song-and-dance number like nothing was wrong:

"Let the stormy clouds chase everyone from the place,

Come on with the rain, I've a smile on my face!"

Our poor classmates were too shocked to do anything but stare in horror. And Clementine and I were all out of great ideas.

I haven't known Hot Dog for very long. But I do know one thing for sure. He may be a little strange, but he always comes through in the end.

He held his umbrella in the air and zoomed up over the rocket ship. Then he pushed one of his amazing bun buttons and rained! Well, Hot Dog didn't exactly rain. But his bun sure did.

And not just a spring-shower rain, either. We're talking major downpour here!

First Mr. G.'s blazing flames fizzled out. Then his whole rocket ship disintegrated!

Chapter 13

Let's Make a Deal

Hot Dog used his umbrella like a parachute to float back down, Mary Poppins style.

"Like I was sayin'!" he said. "That's some mighty powerful vinegar, all right!"

"Whatever it was, it sure worked!" I said. And I guess Mr. G. agreed.

"Wow! That was outta this world!" he said to Hot Dog. "You gotta hook me up with some of that magic rain! If I had a trick like that, I'd be the most popular guy in Gator-Ville—no doubt!"

"How come he's not rapping anymore?" whispered Clementine.

"Maybe it was the vinegar," I whispered back. "He's acting different all the way around!"

"I'll make you a deal," said Hot Dog. "If you return to Gator-Ville, leave the Terrible Triplets behind, remove the beam barrier so these kids can get back to school and promise never to hurt anyone, I'll give you a lifetime supply of that magic rain."

Mr. G. didn't even stop to think about it. He shook Hot Dog's little hand so hard I thought it was going to fall off!

"Little weenie!" he said, "you've got yourself a deal!"

SHAKe
SHAKe
SHAKe

While Hot Dog filled a bunch of containers with his special Dogzalot vinegar, Mr. G. put together a whole new rocket ship! Clementine and I helped load the containers into the rocket ship, and so did *most* of our classmates.

Felicia, Danny and Marybell Marshall were still too beat up from their crashing-egg experience to carry heavy stuff. And Barfalot, Pigburt and Slugburt were sitting stubbornly in the corner—you know, going on strike for not getting to go to Gator-Ville and all.

Once everything was loaded up, Mr. G. waved good-bye, blasted right through Hot Dog's homemade ceiling and headed for the stars.

"He was different," said Clementine.

"You can say that again!" I agreed.

"No, I mean different from the other aliens we've met," she explained. "The other aliens have all been really—well, *evil!* You know, take-over-the-world-and-get-rid-of-all-the-people kind of evil. But when you get right down to it, I really don't think Mr. G. was such a bad guy. When you get right down to it, Mr. G. was nothing more than a lonely, oversized alligator looking for someone to play with. Plus, you have to admit, he was a pretty decent rapper."

"Wow, Hot Dog was right," I laughed. "You really can find something good in everybody!"

"Correction," Clementine said, turning to look at the Terrible Triplets. "I can find something good in *almost* everybody!"

Hot Dog pushed the forgetting button on his bun, and forgetting mist filled the room. If it worked like the other times, no one would remember a thing about the whole eggy freak show—no one but Clementine and me, that is.

"That was *some fun*, huh, kids?" Hot Dog said, wiping the sweat off his forehead. "Wish I could stay and play, but I've got a special *you know who* waitin' for me back on *you know where!*"

"Do you have any idea what he's talking about?" asked Clementine.

"I could be wrong," I answered, "but I think he might have *a date?*"

Hot Dog gave me a wink, high-fived me and disappeared in a sparkling shower of forgetting mist.

Chapter 14

Recess Is Over

The next thing we knew, we were all back up on the playground at good old Lugenheimer Elementary. Not only had our friends forgotten about everything that just happened, but their bruised and aching bodies were all healed!

"Recess is over! Didn't anybody hear the bell?" asked our teacher, Miss Lamphead. "It rang five minutes ago! What's the matter with you kids? You're all going deaf from listening to that horrible rock 'n' roll music! That's it, isn't it?"

"To tell you the truth, Miss Lamphead," said Clementine, "we've been listening to quite a bit more rap than anything else lately."

Chapter 15

Yummy Sardine-and-Marshmallow-with-Rice-Noodle Sandwiches

I'd like to say that everything ended happily ever after. And that's basically true, except for one *beyond* bad thing. Clementine ended up finding the note I'd written on that candy wrapper. Remember the note I put in her pocket when she wasn't breathing? The note where I promised to eat ten of her super-*sickening* sandwiches if she promised not to die?

"Okay, Bob," she said the very next day at lunch, "here is your first tasty treat direct from Clementine's Café! It's my yummy-nummy sardine, marshmallow and rice-noodle sandwich topped off with a squirt of vinegar! Bob? Where are you going? How do you know you don't like it if you won't even try it? Why are you running away? Come on, Bob! A promise is a promise! Hey! I'm not kidding, Bob! You come back here this minute, or else I'm never, ever helping you deal with another space alien as long as you live! Bob? Bob!!!"

THE END

(for now)

As an award-winning investigative reporter specializing in extraterrestrial activity, **L. Bob Rovetch** has spent hundreds of hours interviewing Bob and helping him record his amazing but true adventures. Ms. Rovetch lives across the Golden Gate Bridge from San Francisco with two perfect children and plenty of pets.

Dave Whamond wanted to be a cartoonist ever since he could pick up a crayon. During math classes he would doodle in the margin of his papers. One math teacher warned him, "You'd better spend more time on your math and less time cartooning. You can't make a living drawing funny pictures." Today Dave has a syndicated daily comic strip, called *Reality Check.* Dave has one wife, two kids, one dog and one kidney. They all live together in Calgary, Alberta.

Look out!
The Dogwash Doggies Are
Coming Your Way!

Just when you thought the world was safe! Arriving in Fall 2007:

Hot Dog and Bob and the Surprisingly Slobbery Attack of the Dogwash Doggies

The adventures of Hot Dog and Bob continue in this bone-chewing new episode! All is going well at the fifth-grade fundraiser until talking dogs from the planet Bowwowwowwow, arrive to take over Earth and turn Bob and his unsuspecting classmates into their pets! Hot Dog and Bob must battle this new lazer-beam-chewie-wielding alien duo to save the world!